Soda and Bonda

For Damayanthi and Lara

Soda and Bonda

ISBN 978-93-5046-988-0
© Niveditha Subramaniam
First published in India, 2018

Published by
Tulika Publishers, 24/1 Ganapathy Colony Third Street, Teynampet, Chennai 600 018, India
email reachus@tulikabooks.com   *website* www.tulikabooks.com

Printed and bound by
Sterling and Quadra Press India Limited, #710, Anna Salai, Nandanam, Chennai 600 035, India

Soda and Bonda

Niveditha Subramaniam

This is Soda.

This is Bonda.

Soda **looks** like a dog
and **feels** like a dog.

Bonda **looks** like a cat...

...but **feels** like a dog.

"You are not a

"Stop licking my *face!*"

"Go away,

Bonda is sad.

"Am I not a dog, too?
Why doesn't Soda understand?"

...where

are

„you?"

"Bonda!"

"You're a great dog, Bonda."

"I know!"